The World of Fashion

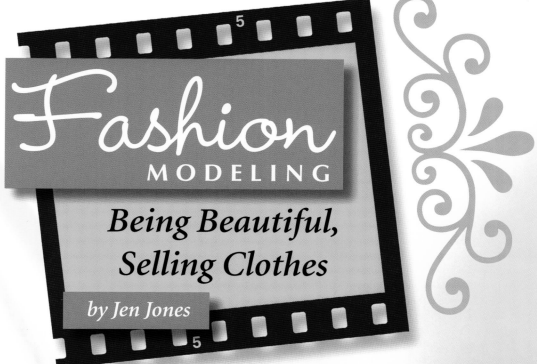

Fashion
MODELING

*Being Beautiful,
Selling Clothes*

by Jen Jones

*Consultant: Lindsay Stewart
Director of the Children's Division
Jet Set Models
La Jolla, California*

Capstone *press*®
Mankato, Minnesota

Snap Books are published by Capstone Press,
151 Good Counsel Drive, P.O. Box 669, Mankato, Minnesota 56002.

www.capstonepress.com

Library of Congress Cataloging-in-Publication Data

Jones, Jen, 1976–

Fashion modeling : being beautiful, selling clothes / by Jen Jones.

p. cm.—(Snap books. The world of fashion)

Summary: "Presents the different types of modeling, how to get
started in modeling, and supermodels of the past and present"—Provided
by publisher.

Includes bibliographical references and index.

ISBN-13: 978-0-7368-6830-3 (hardcover)

ISBN-10: 0-7368-6830-5 (hardcover)

ISBN-13: 978-0-7368-7884-5 (softcover pbk.)

ISBN-10: 0-7368-7884-X (softcover pbk.)

1. Models (Persons)—United States—Juvenile literature. 2. Modeling
agencies—United States—Juvenile literature. I. Title. II. Series.

HD6073.M772U555 2007

746.9'2—dc22

2006021255   2006021258

Editor: Amber Bannerman

Designer: Juliette Peters

Photo Researcher: Charlene Deyle

Photo Credits:
BigStockPhoto.com/Daniel Sroga, 4; Capstone Press/Karon Dubke, 6, 7 (bottom), 16; Corbis/Artiga Photo, 13; Corbis/
Bettmann, 26 (right); Corbis/Corbis/Zack Seckler, 25 (left); Corbis/epa/Olivier Hoslet, cover (left); Corbis/Larry Williams,
23; Corbis/Petre Buzoianu, 24; Corbis/Philip Gould, 17; Corbis/Reuters/Alessandro Bianchi, 9 (bottom left); Corbis/Reuters/
Mike Segar, 14; Corbis/Roger Prigent, 27; Corbis Sygma/Yuste Jose Luis/News Press-Yuste, 28; Corbis/zefa/Ben Welsh,
9 (top right); Getty Images Inc./David Friedman, 10; Getty Images Inc./Evan Agostini, 21; Getty Images Inc./Frazer
Harrison, 7 (top); Getty Images Inc./The Image Bank/Vincent Ricardel, 8; Getty Images Inc./Photographer's Choice/John
Lawrence, 12; Getty Images Inc./Scott Gries, 15; Globe Photos, Inc./Odhams Press, 26 (left); Globe Photos Inc./Sonia
Moskowitz, 29; Michele Torma Lee, 32; PhotoEdit Inc./Barbara Stitzer, 5; PhotoEdit Inc./Jeff Greenberg, 19; Shutterstock/
Iryna Kurhan, cover (right); Shutterstock/Marcus Tuerner, 25 (right); Shutterstock/vm, 20; ZUMA Press/Newday Foto/
Florence Jamart, 18

Table of Contents

Lights, Camera, Glamour

Many young girls dream of being fashion models. Their eyes dance with visions of fame and fortune. For some models, the dream has come true. Just saying the names "Tyra" or "Gisele" sparks instant recognition. For these blessed beauties, million-dollar paydays and adoring admirers are the norm.

Along with perks, modeling has its share of pitfalls. Models face tough competition, loneliness, and rejection. In this book, you'll learn why the business is both glamorous *and* gritty, and what it takes to be successful.

Chapter One

Inside the Biz: Your Passport to the Modeling World

When people think of fashion models, most picture supermodels they've seen in *Vogue* or the Victoria's Secret catalog. But there are more than 95,000 working models just in the United States! Most fashion models are between the ages of 11 and 23. They work in several categories.

Editorial

Magazines hire models to be in fashion spreads and on covers. Since these photos don't advertise a specific product, they are on the lower end of the pay scale. Editorial models start at about $150 per day.

Runway

Designers present new clothing collections at fashion shows. Models strut the runway wearing the designers' clothes. Some runway shows pay models $500 or more per hour.

Catalog

Catalog work isn't as glamorous as other kinds of modeling. But it provides steady work and pays well at $150 to $250 per hour.

Behind the Scenes

You may think that $150 to $500 per hour sounds like a lot of cash. But don't bank on it! Most models don't get paid for their prep time. Traveling, exercising, even eating and sleeping are all things models do to prep for photo shoots. Sound easy? It's not always what it seems. Eight- to twelve- hour days at photo shoots are common. After that, a model usually exercises, eats a healthy meal, and goes to bed. She might have to get up at 6:00 the next morning to start the whole routine again.

Breaking the Mold

High-fashion modeling has very strict rules about looks. However, many other modeling jobs exist for those who aren't young, tall, and thin. If you've got fabulous feet or are blessed with curves, you don't have to give up on a modeling career.

Elegant models must be at least 35 years old. They might be former supermodels or women who appeal to magazines with older readers.

Parts

Models with excellent features might be right for parts modeling. In this type of modeling, certain body parts such as hands, legs, or feet are photographed.

Plus-size

This growing part of the business hires models who wear a size 12 or larger. Yearly salaries can be as much as $200,000.

Landing the Big Break

Does modeling sound like the career for you? If so, you first must figure out a way to "see and be seen." Even picture-perfect looks do a model no good if they go undiscovered. Luckily, there are many ways to get a well-manicured foot in the door.

Model search

Many major agencies launch nationwide model searches. They hope to find "the next big thing." The winner's prize is usually an agency contract or her photo on a magazine cover. After a model signs on with an agency, agents (or "bookers") help her get jobs.

Models also can get their start at conventions. At these large gatherings, model hopefuls meet with and get advice from agents and scouts. Some models even get signed.

Perhaps the most direct route is to attend an open call. At open calls, agencies open their doors to meet new faces.

Scary Scams

A beginning model must be careful to avoid scams. Some businesses take advantage of a model's dreams. They charge lots of money but do nothing to help her career. Agencies that ask you to pay them up front are often committing scams. Respectable agencies only make money *after* a model they represent gets a paid job.

A Whole New World

People model everywhere. But the heart of fashion can be found in Paris, France; Milan, Italy; and New York City. These cities are home to famous models, designers, and fashion shows. A model who is trying to make it usually lands in one of these cities.

Most model hopefuls don't journey to a big city until they've had some success. Industry experts suggest waiting to move until you are at least age 18, and only if you are with a reliable agency.

Adjusting to the high cost of big-city living can be hard. Some agencies pay for new models to live together in dorm-like apartments. Other models take second jobs just to pay the rent. But the excitement of the city and the chance of success often keeps models following their dreams.

Chapter Two

What It Takes: Modeling Must-Haves

Much like the real world, the modeling world is a melting pot. Models of all ethnicities have reached superstardom. Naomi Campbell is known for her exotic beauty. Christie Brinkley has a great All-American look. Then there's the boyish appeal of Kristen McMenamy.

Most models fit into a common body mold. It's rare to see a fashion model shorter than 5 feet, 8 inches tall or larger than a size six. Designers prefer long, slender models because clothing hangs and moves more dramatically on their bodies. Models with a camera-friendly quality that shines from within also appeal to designers.

Naomi Campbell

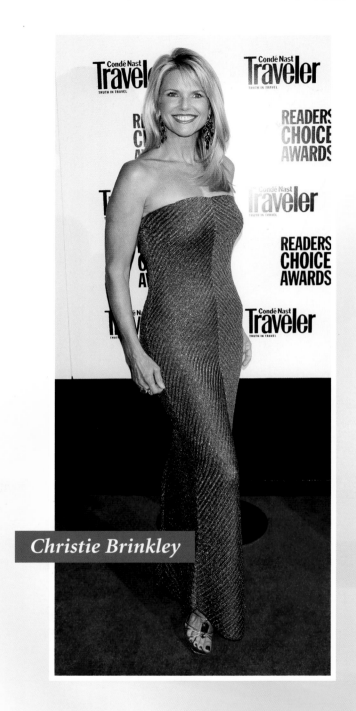

Christie Brinkley

One-Size Doesn't Fit All!

It's important to realize that there are many different body types. Some people are naturally skinny, while others are naturally curvy. Keep your self-esteem high, eat healthy, and exercise regularly. Let your true self shine. Don't let what society is showing us get in the way of your ability to feel beautiful. Be happy with the skin you're in!

Hot Shots

What's the difference between models who work and models who wish? One big factor is comfort and confidence in front of the camera. A model won't succeed if she can't command a photographer's attention. Of course, models have certain tricks for great pictures. Some perfect a pout or pose by practicing in the mirror or taking test shots. Others pretend to be a character in a movie.

Comp card

A model's most important tools are her portfolio and her composite card. The photos inside her portfolio show off her experience, personality, and best physical features. Comp cards include pictures of the model, along with her body stats and agency contacts. Clients look at comp cards and portfolios to see if a model is right for a project.

Oh So Savvy

If you think a model only needs good looks to get by, think again! The length of a model's career depends on many things. She must work well with others and adapt easily to new situations. She also must present herself in the best light possible, especially with new clients. This means taking good care of her health and looks. She must also show up on time and have a friendly attitude.

Successful models also understand the business. Reading fashion magazines and going to runway shows helps models keep current on designers and the hottest new trends.

Reality Check

Just like any lifestyle spent in the spotlight, a modeling career comes with not-so-glitzy drawbacks. It's hard to get ahead, and even when a model does "make it big," she can be terribly lonely. Models travel as much as several weeks per month. Being on the road away from family and friends can be stressful. The competitive nature of the industry often makes it difficult to trust others.

Kate Moss

Eating disorders, drugs, and alcohol abuse are also sadly common among models. Gia Carangi was a popular model in the 1970s. After battling a drug addiction, she died of AIDS in 1986. Kate Moss was photographed using drugs in 2005. Afterward, she lost several high-profile clients. As a model, it's important to keep your morals and self-esteem high. It will then be easier to steer clear of negative traps.

Chapter Three

Role Models: Faces and Figures Who Shape the Industry

Signing an agency contract is the first step to becoming a professional. Agents manage a model's career by landing her go-sees. They also build her portfolio and give her image advice. After taking about 20 percent of a model's earnings, the agency provides a model with her check.

Modeling agencies are found in many cities, but the big players are in New York City. Some of the most well known New York agencies include Ford, Next, IMG, and Elite. Large agencies often are divided into different booking departments. These departments may include men's, women's, parts, and plus-size.

23

Through the Looking Glass

A dazzling magazine spread is the product of talent both in front of and behind the lens. Photographers are the backbone of the business. They frame a model to create the best possible picture. During a photo shoot, a photographer directs a model's poses. Some top models often work with the same photographers. Cindy Crawford got her start working with Victor Skrebneski. Linda Evangelista and photographer Steven Meisel have paired up numerous times for *Vogue*.

Before the photographer starts snapping shots, models spend several hours preparing. Hair and makeup stylists play an important role. Models often spend up to two hours with them.

The VIP of any shoot is the client. The client is on site to approve the work in progress. If a model can impress the client, she may find more work with that company.

Doin' Time

In hopes of getting the perfect shot, some photo shoots can go all day—or all night. Swimsuit models might spend all day in freezing cold water or in the hot sun. Despite these challenges, a model must always keep her cool.

Supermodels of Yesterday

Through the years, models have shaped fashion trends and risen to great fame. The 1960s marked the first time that models became household names. Future actresses Cheryl Tiegs and Cybill Shepherd sported miniskirts. A British model named Twiggy became a celebrity. Many women imitated her "mod" look of short dresses and skirts in bright colors or patterns.

Twiggy, 1960s fashion

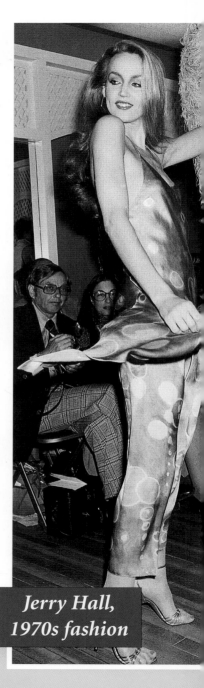

Jerry Hall, 1970s fashion

Carol Alt,
1980s fashion

The 1970s were widely known as the "Halston era." The era was named after the popular disco-style designer Roy Halston Frowick. Models like Jerry Hall and Joan Severance confidently modeled Halston's dresses and pantsuits. During this time, supermodel Janice Dickinson also achieved heights of stardom.

In the 1980s, a variety of cover girls made their mark in the fashion world. They loved the camera as much as it loved them. Supermodels like Christie Brinkley and Carol Alt were spotted everywhere from magazine covers to music videos.

Modern Supermodels

In the 1990s, the top supermodels were very famous. They reached the level of rock stars and actors. Some were known only by their first names: Cindy (Crawford), Claudia (Schiffer), Naomi (Campbell), and Christy (Turlington). Along with this increased celebrity status came more exposure. Singer George Michael featured the era's most famous models in his music video "Freedom." Cindy Crawford completed a popular workout video and hosted MTV's *House of Style*.

Cindy Crawford

Today, pop culture continues to turn models into stars. Milla Jovovich is a model-turned-actress and singer. She has recorded her own music and lit up the screen in movies such as *Zoolander*. *Sports Illustrated* model Heidi Klum hosts fashion reality show *Project Runway*. Another popular show is *America's Next Top Model*. Hosted by Tyra Banks, this show puts the spotlight on new faces.

While not all models reach superstardom, modeling at all levels can be very rewarding. Whether you make it in your hometown or land on the pages of *Elle*, you'll discover the supermodel within. Work it!

agency (AY-juhn-see)—a business that acts on behalf of models or performers

composite card (kuhm-POZ-it KARD)—a card that includes a model's pictures, body statistics, and agency contacts

contract (KON-trakt)—an agreement between a business and a person

go-see (GOH-SEE)—a model's first meeting with a possible client

open call (OH-puhn KAWL)—a casting call that is open to all people

portfolio (port-FOH-lee-oh)—an album of pictures that models use to show agents and clients their experience

Fast Facts

Linda Evangelista's first exposure to modeling was a Miss Teen Canada contest at age 16.

Veronica Webb was discovered while working in a New York City shop.

When she was 15, Naomi Campbell was discovered in London at the tourist shopping hot-spot of Covent Garden.

Gisele Bundchen was first approached by modeling scouts while shopping in a Brazilian mall.

Read More

Levin, Pamela. *Tyra Banks.*
Black Americans of Achievement.
Philadelphia: Chelsea House, 2000.

Rivera, Ursula. *Fashion.* American
Pop Culture. New York: Children's
Press, 2004.

Warrick, Leanne. *Style Trix for
Cool Chix: Your One-Stop Guide to
Finding the Perfect Look.* New York:
Watson-Guptill Publications, 2005.

Internet Sites

FactHound offers a safe, fun way to
find Internet sites related to this book.
All of the sites on FactHound have been
researched by our staff.

Here's how:
1. Visit *www.facthound.com*
2. Choose your grade level.
3. Type in this book ID **0736868305**
   for age-appropriate sites. You may also
   browse subjects by clicking on letters,
   or by clicking on pictures and words.
4. Click on the **Fetch It** button.

**FactHound will fetch the best sites
for you!**

About the Author

Jen Jones has always been fascinated by fashion—and the evidence can be found in her piles of magazines and overflowing closet! She is a Los Angeles-based writer who has published stories in magazines such as *American Cheerleader*, *Dance Spirit*, *Ohio Today*, and *Pilates Style*. She has also written for E! Online and PBS Kids. Jones has been a Web site producer for *The Jenny Jones Show*, *The Sharon Osbourne Show*, and *The Larry Elder Show*. She's also written books for young girls on cheerleading, knitting, figure skating, and gymnastics.

Index